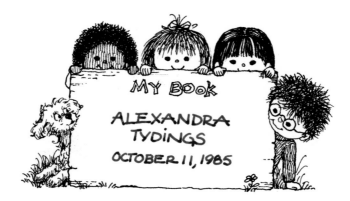

MY BOOK

ALEXANDRA
TYDINGS

OCTOBER 11, 1985

The Magic Show

GYO FUJIKAWA

GROSSET & DUNLAP · PUBLISHERS · NEW YORK

A FILMWAYS COMPANY

Library of Congress Catalog Card Number: 81-80651. ISBN: 0-448-11750-9.

One afternoon, Jenny decided to show
her friends Mei Su, Nicholas, Sam, and Shags the new
things in her dress-up collection.

"Look what I got from Mr. Green," Jenny said.
"He used to be a magician."

"I wish I could be a magician," sighed Sam.

"Pretend to be one," Jenny said.
"Put on Mr. Green's hat and cape, Sam."
"I want to be a real magician," Sam said,
"not a make-believe one. I want to give a real
magic show."
"Maybe there's magic in the cape," Mei Su said.

Nicholas didn't agree.
"That's silly," he said. "How could there
be magic in that beat-up old coat?"
"Put it on anyway, Sam," Jenny said.
"Then do a magic trick."
"Well, I'll try," Sam said.

Sam dropped a green maple leaf into
the magician's hat. He waved his hands over the
hat and said, "PRESTO!" Then Sam reached
into the hat and pulled out a bright red leaf.
   "The leaf turned color!" Jenny said.
   "Magic!" Mei Su said.

"Magic nothing," Nicholas said. "I bet you
put that red leaf in the hat ahead of time, Sam."
"I'm not telling," Sam said. "And now
I'll do some tricks with Shags."

First, Sam snapped
his fingers and Shags
sat up and begged.

When Sam ordered "Speak!"
Shags answered with a bark.

Then Sam yelled, "Bang!"
and Shags rolled over and played dead.

Sam said, "Say your prayers, Shags!"
And Shags did as he was told.

And when Sam said,
  "Dance, Shags, dance!"
Shags pranced on his hind legs.

Finally Sam shouted,
"Sing, Shags, sing for me!"
Shags lifted his head and howled!

Jenny and Mei Su clapped their hands.
"That's wonderful, Sam," they said.

"But it isn't magic," Nicholas said. "It's just
a bunch of dog tricks. Why don't you make
something disappear. Real magicians always
make a rabbit disappear."

"But I don't have a rabbit," Sam said.

"Use something else," Nicholas said.
"How about Mei Su's canary?"

"Oh, no," Mei Su said, "not Coco."

"Sam won't hurt Coco, Mei Su,"
Jenny said. "Come on. Let's all go
to Mei Su's house."

The four friends ran to Mei Su's.
There, Coco was singing happily
in his cage.

"I don't know exactly how
to make Coco disappear," Sam said.

"If Mei Su takes Coco out of
the cage," Jenny said, "you could
wave your hands over him and say
'Presto.' Maybe that will work."

"And maybe it won't," Nicholas said.
Mei Su opened the cage door
and brought the little canary out
on her finger. But when Sam began to
wave his hands, Coco got frightened
and flew right out the window.

"Somebody catch Coco!" Mei Su cried.
Everybody raced outside. They were just in time
to see the little bird flying towards the woods.
Then Coco disappeared.
"We've got to get him back!" Sam said.

They looked for Coco everywhere.
They looked around the frog pond.

They looked along the paths
and in the woods where the squirrels
and the woodpeckers lived.

They looked in bushes and in trees.
But there was no sign of Coco anywhere.
"Maybe we'd better go home and see
if we can get someone to help us,"
Jenny said sadly.
"I think so, too," Nicholas said.
But Sam didn't want to give up.

"I'm going to keep on looking," he said.

All of a sudden Sam saw a yellow feather on the ground. "Coco must be nearby," he thought. Sam looked up — and there, perched on a branch right over his head was Coco!

"I've found him! I've found him!" Sam yelled to his friends. And they all came running back.

"Oh, Sam," Mei Su said, "you found Coco."

"How are we going to get him to come down?"
Nicholas asked.

Sam thought for awhile. Then he whispered
to Mei Su and she ran off. In a few minutes
she was back with Coco's cage and a box of the
canary's favorite birdseed.

Sam put the cage on the ground and opened
the door. He scattered a trail of Coco's food
that led right into his cage.

"Call Coco to come down and eat, Mei Su,"
Sam said.

"Come down, Coco," Mei Su called.
"Please come down. Your dinner's ready."

Coco left the branch and flew around.
Then he fluttered to the ground and began to eat
the seeds. Coco kept on eating along the trail
of birdseed until he hopped right through the cage door.
Sam quickly closed it behind him.

"You got Coco back in his cage," Mei Su said.
"Oh, Sam! Thank you!"

"What made you think of using the seeds
to get Coco back into the cage?" Nicholas asked Sam.
"Well," Sam said, "I remembered that when
I'm hungry I go home to eat. Coco's home is his cage."
"That was a real trick," Jenny said.
"Yes," Nicholas said. "But it wasn't magic."
"It was to me," Mei Su said. "It took real magic
to get Coco back."

"I think you deserve a medal, Sam," Jenny said. . . .
"And I'm going to give you one."